The purple tiger

LILY BARRASS

Published by BookPublishingWorld 2021

Copyright © Lily Barrass 2021

ISBN 978-1-8381944-9-9

BookPublishingWorld
is an imprint of
Dolman Scott Ltd
www.dolmanscott.co.uk

For Sophie and Sarah,
With love, Lily

In a small town, called Abberliegers,
  Lives a large group of beautiful tigers .

ROAR!

They have amazing stripes and lovely roars,
And an unusual pattern on their paws.

One day Tilda the tiger had a huge announcement,
That she was going to have three little Cubs.

I have some news....

And as the days drew closer and closer,
The excitement grew and grew,
And the preparation for the Cubs began,
And was over before you knew.

Eventually the time had come,

For Tilda to meet her Cubs.

But something was different about the third
born, Rue,

As she was born purple, and had unique stripes.

She only has three legs, and her ears are very pointy,

But her tail is very long and fluffy,
unlike her brothers, theirs are scruffy.

11

She was beautiful,

12

inside and out.

13

Her amazing eyes,
were the colour of the skies,
And shone very bright,
Like all the stars above.

She played all day with the other tigers,

But mostly her best friends, Sarah and Sophie.

They liked playing tag and hide and seek,

18

And read lots of books, like little bow peep.

They ran around, and had lots of fun.
And when the sun went down, they waved
goodbye

At night they slept in a cozy den,
Until it was time to play again.
They huddled up all nice and tight, and had
lovely dreams throughout the night.

One day, a tiger called Oscar came over to Rue and asked,

Why are you purple and why have you only got three legs?

Tilda replied,
"It makes her special, the colour of her skin may be different to yours Oscar, but she is just like us really. She does the same and eats the same as us. And she run just as fast as you, even with three legs. She doesn't let anything stop her."

So all the other tigers realised that the way you look doesn't define you, and learnt not to judge for the way people look.

For Rue, the tiger was loved by all, and that was all that matters.

CPSIA information can be obtained
at www.ICGtesting.com
Printed in the USA
BVHW021354010621
608554BV00005B/750

9 781838 194499